ELVIN LINK,
PLEASE REPORT TO THE PRINCIPAL'S OFFICE!

ELVIN LINK,
PLEASE REPORT TO THE
PRINCIPAL'S
OFFICE!

DREW DERNAVICH

Christy Ottaviano Books
HENRY HOLT AND COMPANY · NEW YORK

Henry Holt and Company, *Publishers since 1866*
Henry Holt® is a registered trademark of Macmillan Publishing Group, LLC
120 Broadway, New York, NY 10271
mackids.com

Library of Congress Cataloging-in-Publication Data

Names: Dernavich, Drew, author, illustrator.
Title: Elvin Link, please report to the principal's office / Drew Dernavich.
Description: First edition. | New York : Christy Ottaviano Books, Henry Holt and
    Company, 2020. | Summary: A penchant for doodling often lands fifth-grader
    Elvin Link in the principal's office, but also helps with crime-solving and
    standing up to bullies.
Identifiers: LCCN 2019018542 | ISBN 978-1-62779-209-7 (hardcover : alk.
    paper) | ISBN 978-1-250-11933-9 (ebook)
Subjects: | CYAC: Middle schools—Fiction. | Schools—Fiction. |
    Doodles—Fiction. | Family life—Fiction. | Mystery and detective stories.
Classification: LCC PZ7.1.D475 Elv 2020 | DDC [Fic]—dc23
LC record available at https://lccn.loc.gov/2019018542

Our books may be purchased in bulk for promotional, educational, or business
use. Please contact your local bookseller or the Macmillan Corporate and
Premium Sales Department at (800) 221-7945 ext. 5442 or by email at
MacmillanSpecialMarkets@macmillan.com.

First edition, 2020

Printed in the United States of America by LSC Communications,
Harrisonburg, Virginia

1 3 5 7 9 10 8 6 4 2

FOR LINDSEY AND CARTER

CHAPTER 1

I have a question for you.

Which would you rather sit at: the command center of a spaceship or a boring old school desk?

It's the spaceship, right? I thought so. Me too!

Now that that's out of the way, let me tell you something about me. My name is Elvin Link. I'm in fifth grade. I like to draw. I mean, I *really* like to draw. I'll

draw humans, animals, monsters, aliens, half human–half chickens, you name it. I don't even need paper. As long as the surface is flat, I'll draw on anything: walls, floors, clothes, furniture, whatever. I like to draw at home, on the bus, at school, and on vacation. And I'll draw with anything: pens, pencils, markers, chalk, crayons, brushes, or erasers. You never know what you might need or when you might need it, so I've always got drawing stuff in my backpack:

pencils & pens

erasers

notebooks

paper

markers

sharpener

crayons

chalk

allergic!

not allergic but still don't like

too Loud!

There are a bunch of things I don't like: team sports, peanuts, bees, motorcycles, hot-air balloons, clothes shopping, doctors' offices, and cleaning supplies.

not too fond of heights

But, as I said, I do like to draw.

That's why I decided to turn my boring old desk at school into a spaceship. Check it out: the swivel laser cannon, the auxiliary rocket engines, even the rocket-fueled legs! This was going to be a fully functioning extraterrestrial vehicle. And it was something I would have been far more excited to sit at than my boring earthbound desk.

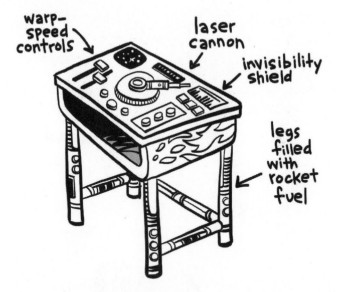

In other words, this might have been the coolest thing ever.

Here's who didn't agree: my teacher, Mrs. English.

Mrs. English

None of my teachers approve of my drawing on surfaces other than paper. But I like Mrs. English, which is why this was a bummer. As teachers go, she's pretty cool.

Here are a few things you should know about her:

1. She lives on a farm.
2. She likes to teach math. So why is this her name?
3. She can't see. Well, what I mean is that she has really poor eyesight and wears glasses that are as thick as a pair of ice cubes.

That last fact is also why she writes in REALLY BIG letters. And on this particular day, she wrote this on the whiteboard:

I was excited about the planet thing. Who doesn't like imagining what it would be like to live on another planet? The part about getting into teams and looking up information together in books or online—not quite as interesting.

So, as my group was getting organized, and discussing which planet we were going to look at, and deciding how to split up the work, it occurred to me that the best way to get to know a planet would be to go there. And to go there, you'd need a spaceship.

Which is why I turned my desk into one.

The funny thing is, when Mrs. English saw it, she didn't even know what it was.

"Elvin! Why did you turn your desk into a piñata?"

A piñata? I knew Mrs. English had vision issues, but wow! If I'm going to get in trouble for drawing on my desk, it better be for an awesome space vehicle, not a pony covered in crepe paper. In the end, though, it didn't matter what Mrs. English thought it was.

"I will see you in the principal's office immediately after school, Mr. Link."

This was not the first time I'd been in trouble for drawing on things. I'm a regular in after-school detention, so they might as well name it after me.

In fact, it's where I met Carlos, who is my best friend. But more on him later.

Here's who else didn't go for my desk spaceship: well, a lot of people, actually. And they lined up in the principal's office after school to tell me. Mrs. English went first.

Because sometimes pictures say things better than words?

Mr. Trinkle, a science teacher, went next.

I hadn't "defaced" a tray. I'd drawn *utensils that were way cooler!* But this was not my time to talk.

Next was the school principal, Principal Weeks.

cooler utensils

food plow

fwhistle

fidget spooner

And remember when you drew a cityscape all over the lockers? That has no place here.

One more incident and you'll have to go to summer school.

The cityscape had been for a class project. The lockers basically look like the outlines of buildings, so I added some details.

Wait. Did Principal Weeks say summer school? *Summer school!* There was only one kid I knew who had gone to summer school: Peter Zorber. I didn't want to be like him.

"We've got a project for you, Elvin," Principal Weeks continued. "Some people keep a daily journal or diary. They write down things that are important to them: their thoughts, their feelings, or even just stuff they find interesting. Whenever you feel inspired to draw something on a wall or a locker or a tray, we'd like you to draw it here instead. And we'd like you to do that from now until the end of the school year."

Turdmuffins, I thought.

Or maybe I said it out loud.

"Elvin!" Principal Weeks said, handing me a blank notebook. "Put that in here."

"You can draw whatever you're feeling, Elvin—anything, good or bad. You won't get in trouble for it. But if you're going to stay out of summer school, you've got to keep your drawings in this journal. Understood?"

The school janitor, Mr. Torres, was also there. He had carried my desk all the way to Principal Weeks's office. It was his turn to speak, but he didn't say anything.

He just handed me cleaning supplies and nodded at me and then at the desk. I didn't have to ask what the nods meant. I don't cheat or steal or swear or push kids down the stairs. I draw. Drawing is good, right? How could it be that the one good thing I liked was going to ruin my life?

What might have seemed like the beginning of the worst week ever turned out to be the best. This is the story of how that happened.

With pictures, naturally.

CHAPTER 2

It was the end of the school year, when all that was on our minds (besides summer, of course) was Field Day. Exactly one week from today.

On every other school day, we're either doing multiplication tables or reading about Thomas Edison. Or worse, both.

Field Day is different. Everybody gets to go outside and compete in all kinds of games and sports. There are always two teams, the Blue Team and the Gold Team, based on the two main colors of the Villadale town flag.

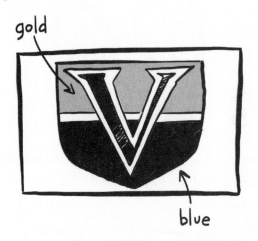

gold

blue

Today was the day the team lists were posted. At the end of the day, everyone ran to the front entrance to find out their teams. Then everybody went outside to the parking lot, where Eazy Freezy,

the ice cream truck, was serving up scoops.

Well, everybody but me. Instead of hanging outdoors

and eating mint chocolate chip, I was hunched over a desk, breathing cleaning fumes in the principal's office.

This was especially difficult for me because I really needed Field Day to happen. Or I guess it's more accurate to say that I really needed Field Day to be over with.

That's because I was

You know That Kid: the one person who does something so completely embarrassing that everybody talks about it like . . .

And that's how people remember you for the summer: not by name, but by the fact you did that amazingly stupid thing. You don't want to be That Kid.

The legends of previous That Kids are almost as popular as Field Day itself. For instance, a boy named Zach Walker once vomited on a balloon *during* the water balloon toss and then tried to *toss the balloon to somebody else*—as if anybody would touch an exploding puke bomb! He is now known as Yak Walker.

Two years ago, Clarissa Gomez and Mai Lin Lee ran in the three-legged race, shrieking while holding their noses. As they fell across the finish line and wriggled out of the sack, they found that a frightened squirrel inside it had pooped on their feet in terror. The squirrel was okay, but the girls got teased about it forever.

But instead of being That Kid, they were Those Girls, so at least they had each other.

Unfortunately, I was That Kid last year. It happened at the Gatorade relay. That's a relay where you run back and forth with cups of water and pour them into a bucket filled with powdered Gatorade. Once the bucket is full, you have to mix it, pour it back into the cups, and drink it. Whichever team drinks the full bucket first wins.

I was the first one to run. I tripped and did a massive face-plant into the blue powdered Gatorade. (It's always the blue kind and the yellow kind, because of our school colors.)

I was already sweaty, so the blue powder stuck like glue. I couldn't see well, obviously, and I stumbled around for a few moments, trying to figure out where I was. I didn't get a nickname, but people said I looked like a tranquilized Smurf.

my face

And they had to do the race over because everybody was laughing too hard to continue. So last summer I had to live with the fact that in the final memory anybody had of me, I looked like a stumbling zombie who had been hit with a blueberry pie. But it couldn't happen two years in a row, right? Surely there would be a new That Kid this year. I needed this to happen. I needed a new team, new teammates, new memories.

"Don't forget the legs, too, Elvin," Principal Weeks said. "I want the whole desk spotless before I let you go."

At this moment, scrubbing the desk in the principal's office made me feel like I was always going to be

THAT KID.

CHAPTER 3

f the desk could have talked, it would have said

But I finally finished cleaning it back to its boring old self.

"There's still time to catch the Eazy Freezy truck," Principal Weeks said. "So why don't you check the list to find out your team, then get an ice cream. And, Elvin . . ."

she really didn't
pause this long but
to me it felt
super tense
and seemed like
it lasted forever
and this is the
only way I can
show that

"Well, let's just say, don't let this happen again."
Message received.
I left Principal Weeks's office and headed to the front
entrance, where I found my name on the Gold Team.

New year, new color. That was a good sign.

Then I made my way outside. I could tell by the lack of noise that the crowd had thinned out. It sounded suspiciously quiet.

When I arrived at the parking lot, I saw a scene that looked like this:

The ice cream truck was there, and a few groups of kids were scattered around. In the middle of the parking lot, Mrs. English and Mr. Trinkle were staring down at a splattered ice cream cone. Principal Weeks came outside and joined them. They all looked pretty angry.

"I don't know what just happened," Mrs. English said. "I got my cone, and as I turned around, someone plowed into me and knocked it out of my hand."

"Are those yours?" Principal Weeks asked, pointing at the ground.

but at least not angry at **me**

Poor Mrs. English. *Adios, glasses!*

"Did you see what happened, Steve?" Principal Weeks asked, but Mr. Trinkle didn't say anything. He seemed more interested in his mountain of fudge caramel swirl.

Principal Weeks raised her voice and asked the kids outside, "Did anyone see who knocked into Mrs. English?"

They didn't see, or they didn't want to tell. It was probably the second one. Either way, there was one frustrated principal, one upset teacher, one pair of broken glasses, and two splattered scoops of cherry ice cream on the ground.

"I'm very disappointed no one is coming forward—accident or not," Principal Weeks snapped. "Field Day is coming up. There will be consequences."

Here's how I would describe the scene:

I wanted a mint chocolate chip cone, but it seemed like the wrong time to ask. Some kids were standing still, silently finishing their last few licks. A few teachers were standing in a half-circle with their hands on their hips. Nobody knew what to do. Neither did I. So I stared down at the ice cream splatter.

It was a cool shape. I imagined it as a flying slime monster with wings and a tail.

Nobody was talking. Let's face it—I was bummed out. It's sad to see ice cream splattered on the ground, especially when you didn't get the chance to have any.

Since the ice cream was starting to melt, I opened my backpack, found my chalk, and traced the outline of the spill on the pavement. I wanted to preserve the memory of the ice cream.

When the police think somebody has been murdered, they draw a chalk outline around the body so that they can continue to analyze the scene after the body has been removed. I guess I learned it from movies, because nothing like this has ever happened in Villadale.

Then again, I might have learned it from my father. He's a police officer.

CHAPTER 4

Meet my dad. Or, as he's known in town, Officer Link.

his badge

my dad

It's cool having a police officer for a father, but maybe not in the way you'd guess. When people think of the police, they call up images of high-speed car chases and shootouts at abandoned warehouses—things like that. Nonstop action.

In reality, though, it's more like this:

Villadale is a medium-size town where people know each other. The criminals are mostly just regular people who do dumb things. And the police are mostly regular people, too, just trying to keep the town safe and peaceful. My dad is one of them.

I've observed a thing or two about problem-solving from him. Case in point . . .

"You can tell by the shape of the splatter that the cone fell *like this*," I said, pointing to the wings of the slime monster. "So whoever ran into Mrs. English was running in that direction."

Principal Weeks looked stunned that I actually said something useful. "That's a good observation, Elvin," she said. "Can you tell us anything else?"

The guy in the Eazy Freezy truck finally spoke up.

"I saw who did this," he said, once he had our attention. "There were a bunch of kids all running around and chasing each other, and one of them knocked into the teacher. I don't know his name, but I saw what he looked like. I could describe his face."

When someone sees a crime happen, the police often ask the person to describe what the culprit looks like so they can draw a picture of the suspect. It's called a composite sketch. The person who draws the face based on the description is called a sketch artist.

"I can draw him!" I responded.

I had never actually done this before, but I thought it might be cool to try. It involved drawing, after all. It wasn't until after I suggested the idea that I thought, *Uh-oh, this could turn me into a snitch.*

On the other hand, I realized, this might put me on the good side of the teachers, at least for a moment.

"Great," said Principal Weeks. "What do we have to lose? Let's go back to my office and set you up."

The principal's office. So many great memories there!

(sarcasm)

"Do you have everything you need, Elvin?" Principal Weeks asked.

Everything I needed to draw? Of course I did. But there was one thing I was missing.

"Can I have three scoops of mint chocolate chip first?"

Didn't happen.

CHAPTER 5

"**H**e was around your height, but heftier than you."

I was sitting in the principal's office, across from the Eazy Freezy man, sketching as he spoke. Principal Weeks and Mr. Trinkle stood next to us, watching but not interfering.

I knew the word heft meant "weight." If somebody was hefty, they were kind of bigger.

"His face was round, with curly brownish hair," the ice cream truck guy continued. "Not brown, but not black, either."

I started with light pencil first, then darkened it once I thought it looked right.

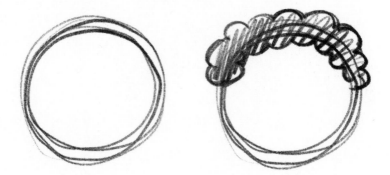

"The curls went down lower, to his eyebrows."

"What kind?" I asked. "Tight curls, or the big, floppy ones?"

"The floppy kind."

"He had a bulbous nose," he continued. "It was distinctive." Bulbous means it's wide and round, and easy to draw. I know that word because an uncle of mine has a nose that he's described as bulbous.

"His eyes were close together and set deep behind his eyebrows, if you know what I mean." I did. If a person has deep-set eyes, that means more of them are covered in shadows.

"He had a normal mouth and red plumpy cheeks, I suppose. Maybe because he was running."

Ears? I asked him about those. He said he hadn't seen them because of the hair, so I didn't draw that part. It's not easy drawing a face from somebody's description, but I was doing my best.

"Like this?" I said.

"Yeah, that looks a lot like the kid," he said. "You're on the right track." The face was starting to appear familiar to me—and not in a good way.

"What was he wearing?" asked Principal Weeks.

"A T-shirt—gray or blue, something like that. It had a number on it. I'm pretty sure it was a one. Like from a sports uniform."

I know exactly what those numbers look like. They're big and blocky on the ends.

"Yeah, that's pretty good," he said. "*Really* good, actually!"

"It looks good to me, too," Principal Weeks said.

It was a great likeness. I was happy with how the drawing had turned out, but I wasn't happy about the realization.

Because I knew I had just drawn a picture of my best friend, Carlos.

"I think I know who this is," Principal Weeks said. "Do you?"

"I do," I answered. I didn't say his name, but she knew that I knew.

"I'll need to speak to this person on Monday."

"*Turdmuffins*," I mumbled.

Principal Weeks smiled and motioned to my journal.

I turned a page and doodled:

CHAPTER 6

When I got home, I was pretty excited to talk to my mother about my day. I especially couldn't wait to get to the part about being a sketch artist. But her face was speaking louder than I was.

Obviously, Principal Weeks had called Mom about the desk. My dad may be a police officer, but it's my mom who lays down the law in our household.

"No summer camp for you, Elvin. It's going to be summer school."

Whatever, I thought. I wouldn't necessarily miss camp. The only thing that made it fun was that Carlos was there, too.

"Go to your room until I call you to set the dinner table."

I didn't like being sent to my room. But I also didn't mind being in my room. There, I could draw without fear of being punished.

Plus, I wasn't alone. I had Otto.

Otto is a betta fish that I won at a fair last year. Well, that *we* won.

Carlos and I had been throwing beanbags, trying to sink Mr. Trinkle (he asks kids to call him Steve because he wants to seem cool) at the dunking booth, when we heard "Last call for entries!" over the loudspeaker.

There was a contest to see who could guess how many jelly bears were in this big jar. Carlos didn't want the fish—he just wanted to see if we could guess correctly.

I first wrote down 358, but Carlos didn't like that number.

He scribbled it out and wrote 1,004, but I definitely disagreed with that.

I scribbled that out and wrote 417. Of course, Carlos thought it was still too low, so he scratched that number out as well. We went back and forth this way until there was no more room to write. What a mess.

Panicking, Carlos said, "It's last call, Elvin!" I reached over to get a new piece of paper, but Carlos grabbed our entry form and shoved it into the box.

"Sometimes you just gotta react," Carlos said, shrugging his shoulders.

Mrs. Rho announced the winner:

But when she opened the jar to count the jelly bears, just to make sure that the count was correct, this is what happened:

They had all melted together into one giant brick. The teachers couldn't pull them apart, so it was impossible to confirm the actual number. That's when Carlos did some quick thinking.

"The number is one!" Carlos yelled. "We got it right!"

He retrieved our entry form and held it up. From a distance (and turned vertical), it did look a lot like a one—a big, fat, messy number one, his favorite number.

"Good enough for me," Mrs. Rho said. "You guys are the winners!"

So Otto was my fish, but Carlos won him for me, which was cool.

People say that fish aren't great pets. Otto may not be as fun as a dog, but I like him. I'm kind of jealous of Otto, too. He's a fighting fish, alone in his tank with nobody to fight.

The Ottoman Empire →

But that also means there's nobody to bother him.

I needed to draw, so I pulled out my journal. I imagined what it might be like to swim in my own tank, just like Otto, surrounded by things. It didn't include any kind of cleaning products.

out for a run, which is what she typically does on a Saturday morning.

Today my dad was making blueberry pancakes. He likes loading up the pancakes with extra treats. Which is why I was surprised when I sat down at the table to an empty plate.

"No pancakes?" I asked.

"Based on your activities yester-day, no. That's according to your mom."

"Not even plain?"

"Not even plain."

In our house we were granted different pancake rights depend-ing on our behavior during the week. My status was the one you don't want.

"But I helped Principal Weeks identify the—"

CHAPTER 7

No matter how bad things got during the week, there were always pancakes to look forward to on Saturday morning.

My dad doesn't usually like to cook unless it involves fire.

Pancakes were his one exception. My mom was

"You're lucky she is allowing you to participate in Field Day."

As if eating cereal wasn't bad enough, I had to eat cereal that made fun of me.

That's what was written on the Post-it note that tumbled out of the box.

I hate being called Baby Bro for two reasons.

Reason #1 → Andrea

Reason #2 → Amanda

Or maybe reason #1 is Amanda and reason #2 is Andrea. Put them in whichever order you want. They're my identical twin sisters, and they like to say "Baby Bro" in that sarcastic way that makes it seem like they don't really care if they have a brother or not, because they have each other. They are only thirteen months older than I am, but they make me pay for it. They also go to my school, since it goes up to sixth grade.

It's funny that they're called "identical" twins, because they're opposite in a lot of ways. But I guess that's true of all family members: everybody is different. There are some things family members have in common.

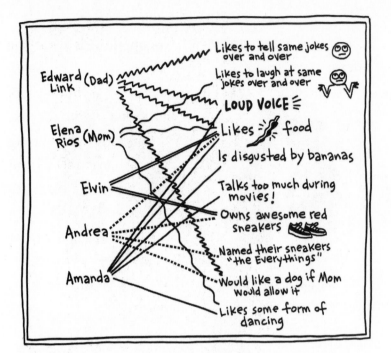

Edward Link (Dad)

Elena Rios (Mom)

Elvin

Andrea

Amanda

Likes to tell same jokes over and over

Likes to laugh at same jokes over and over

LOUD VOICE

Likes 🌶 food

Is disgusted by bananas

Talks too much during movies!

Owns awesome red sneakers 👟

Named their sneakers "the Everythings"

Would like a dog if Mom would allow it

Likes some form of dancing

Another thing my sisters have in common is that they love to prank me. Andrea and Amanda were looking down, knowing that I had seen the Post-it note, but they still kept straight faces.

Andrea is pretty good at looking down, because she loves reading. She has her face buried in a book a lot. She is also fascinated with insects. (She calls herself a scientist, but I think it's better to say she just likes bugs.) Staring into a book with grasshopper diagrams or peering at a butterfly through a microscope lens is what she enjoys.

On the other hand, Amanda is good at looking up.  Usually it's at theater lights, because she likes to be onstage, singing or acting. (She calls herself an actor, but I think it's better to say that she just likes it when people look at her.) Since she has experience acting, she was pretty convincing as she ate her pancakes. She flipped her head to the side and then started to sing.

♫ da da ♪
dee da ♫
da da da
♪♫ dummmm
♫

Which was the melody of whatever show tune she was currently obsessed with. This was irritating. It was also overacting. She was trying too hard. She was the one who'd written the stupid Post-it note, I was sure.

Andrea had brought her final class project to the table, a papier-mâché moth that she carried around everywhere and called Mothy. She was looking at the statue but had a smirk on her face. That wasn't like her. Maybe the Post-it note had been her idea?

The reality is that Andrea and Amanda probably wrote it together. They do this all the time. Whichever one I accuse, the other says:

And then they try to act innocent and avoid punishment. They love doing this, because even if they both get punished, at least they have the satisfaction of knowing that they fooled people.

Sisters, am I right?!

"I bet there are some pancakes in your spaceship," Amanda piped up, giggling with Andrea.

"That's enough, girls," my dad said. "You want me to exchange those for plain pancakes?"

The girls put their heads down and finished up.

"I heard you're all on the same Field Day team this year," my dad continued. "I'd like to see you root for each other for a change."

CHAPTER 8

We want to do something special with our shirts again this year," Andrea said. "Bedazzle them, maybe. Make them different from each other."

Every student gets a T-shirt for Field Day—a gold shirt or a blue one, with a number on the back.

this shirt is BLUE

and this shirt is GOLD

The school gives them to us the day before Field Day so that people can decorate them if they like— stickers, patches, buttons. Last year, for some reason, the teachers decided it would be a good idea to separate the twins—one on the Gold Team, one on the Blue Team. My sisters didn't really go for that. Amanda took her gold shirt and cut it in half, and Andrea took her blue shirt and did the same. They had my mom stitch them together so they each had a half-blue, half-gold shirt. Or, as they told everybody:

Get it?

"Maybe you can help them, Elvin," my father said. "Put that talent to good use. That would be a cool thing to do, right?"

None of us were sure who that comment was directed to.

My mom came through the front door, looking sweaty but happy. "How are the pancakes today?"

"Why don't you see for yourself," my dad said, smiling. He handed her a plate with the last of the blueberry pancakes. "Elvin isn't the only artist in this house."

I didn't need to watch my parents eat pancakes together. I decided it was a good time to take the garbage out—my Saturday chore. Walking back to the house, I saw a giant centipede on the sidewalk. Andrea would be fascinated by this, I thought.

I almost stepped on it. But didn't.

Instead, I drew a chalk outline around the centipede.

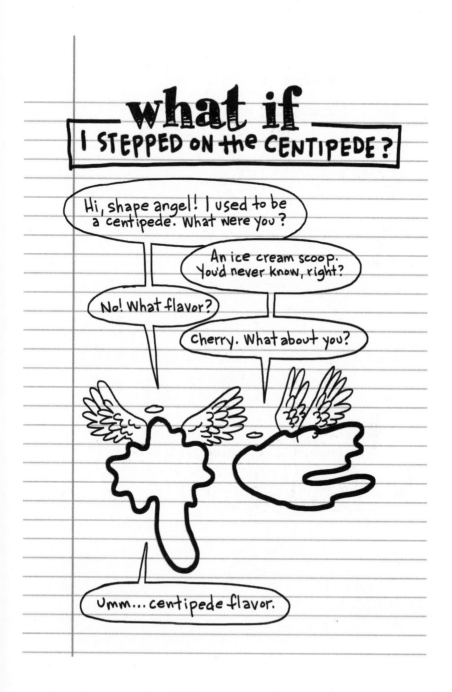

CHAPTER 9

That afternoon, Carlos came over. He was wearing another number one shirt.

"Number One Suspect" is what popped into my head.

Carlos is bigger and more active than I am. Notice that I didn't say athletic—just active. The fact that my father is a police officer is exciting to Carlos. He thinks it's the coolest job in the world.

"What up, Mr. L! Chased any bank robbers lately?" Carlos said as he walked through the door and did some action-movie poses in front of my dad.

"I'll let you know when I catch them, Carlos."

"Awesome! Then I can ride around in a cruiser with you."

"Be careful what you wish for," Dad said as he picked up the vase and flowers.

On Monday, Carlos was going to get sent to detention—or worse—for being Mrs. English's glasses smasher-and-runner. He would eventually find out that it was because of the drawing I had done.

is what I was thinking.

is what I said instead. I prefer games over difficult conversations.

Carlos and I invented flipdisc. The rules are easy: it's basically just throwing a Frisbee back and forth. But right before you catch it, the thrower gets to name what the Frisbee actually is, and so you have to make a quick decision whether it's something you want to catch . . .

. . . or not.

The identity of the disc can flip in a second, hence the name.

I let Carlos throw first.

And then it was my turn.

"I saw that you're on the Gold Team for Field Day,"

Carlos said, releasing the Frisbee. "That's a bummer! *Peanut-butter-and-Fluff-flavored vegetables!*"

"I know," I said. "I wish we were on the same team. But I'm glad I don't have to look at the blue Gatorade again." *Pez container full of tiny puppies!*"

"Aw, who even remembers that?" Carlos said. "Hey, were you at the ice cream truck yesterday? *Screaming jellyfish that pulls your ears off!*"

"I had to go to the principal's office. *Principal's office!*"

"Why did you catch it?" I yelled.

"You didn't name it," he answered.

"I did. Principal's office!"

"That doesn't count!" he protested. "You were just repeating yourself!"

"I was naming something nasty!"

"Okay, new rule: you can't repeat yourself, or else you're the one who has to touch it."

"Done."

"Why were you there? *Zombie whose skin is covered in toenails!*"

"I drew a spaceship on my desk. But Principal Weeks made me stay late and scrub it off. *Invisible time-traveling school desk!*"

"That's the worst." He laughed. "You missed it! I told Todd Quintilla that if he could grab the cone out of my hand, I'd do his homework for the rest of the year. So he and a bunch of others started running after me, but I dodged 'em all! I was like BING BANG BOOM and left them in the dust! And then I ran all the way home. It was spectacular!"

It did sound spectacular, even if he was unaware of the other side of the story.

"Throw the Frisbee!" I said.

Carlos unleashed the disc. *"A hu-mongous, gigantic bird! Like a super-eagle! It's big, bigger than an airplane! But instead of a regular beak, it has this giant robotic beak made out of pure metal, which . . ."*

I let the Frisbee drop. "You took too long," I shouted. "How am I supposed to know if that's a cool thing?"

wump

"It was gonna be!"

"New rule: one word only!"

"One word?" Carlos said. "That's kinda pathetic."

"Just for today," I yelled as I tossed the Frisbee back. *"Diarrrheeeaaaa!"*

"Video games?" Carlos shouted after retrieving the disc from the ground and throwing it back.

"Nope! That's two words," I said.

"No, I meant—do you want to play video games instead?"

Sounded like a good plan to me.

CHAPTER 10

Before Carlos left, we had to uphold a certain tra-dition that we also invented. This one didn't have a name.

We like to make our own nachos. At first glance, they look normal enough:

Well, normal for *us*.

We have a friendly competition whenever we're eating nachos. Whoever is hosting gets to make them.

And we season them as hot and spicy as we can, using any secret ingredients we have at our disposal.

Then we start eating chips, taking turns. Chip by chip, mouthful by mouthful. But without any water or any kind of drink to cool our mouths off. The battle is to see who can last the longest. If you can make it through the pile of nachos without drinking, you are the champion. We are pretty even at this, although Carlos sweats more.

Since we were at my house, I got to create the masterpiece. Not only did I jam it full of jalapeños and chiles, but I had a bottle of this stuff:

It didn't seem too hot at first, but it had a slow burn that got more and more intense. Before we knew it, our mouths were on fire. But neither of us wanted to be the first to break.

The contest was on.

"I want to set the school record for the beanbag toss at Field Day," Carlos said, fanning his mouth. The beanbag toss wasn't an entirely accurate name. It was a beanbag chair—the big, squishy kind—that we had to throw for distance.

"I know I can do it. I almost did it last year." His face was redder than a tomato as he reached for his next chip.

"I know. You were so close!" I wondered: Would they *really* prevent Carlos from participating in Field Day? He would be so upset. My mouth was now on fire, and it felt like the fire was spreading to the back of my eyeballs. "I just want to make it through Field Day without falling on my face," I said before eating the next chip.

"I've been practicing in the woods behind my house with a bag of wet, dirty laundry." He was sweating so much he looked like Niagara Falls. "You'll cheer me on, right? Even though you're on the Gold Team?"

"Yep," I said, even though I couldn't feel my lips. I did want him to break the beanbag toss record. I suddenly felt horrible that he might be kept from participating, like it would be my fault, and he'd be angry at me. My head felt like hot candle wax ready to drip down my body. That didn't help. I stuffed the next molten-lava chip into my burning mouth.

Carlos looked like he had been stung in the face by a thousand bees.

"It's going . . ."

"To . . ."

"Be . . ."

"Awesome," he finally breathed, like a panting dog, totally oblivious to the conflict going on in my head. He put the next chip on his tongue like he was applying a Band-Aid.

"I know!" I said. I could barely get the words out. "We're both gonna . . ."

I didn't know which was worse: feeling like I could melt steel with my burning tongue, or picturing Carlos sitting inside the school while everybody else was out enjoying Field Day. I was on the edge of breaking.

I broke. But not by drinking.

I think they're going to keep you out of Field Day!

Carlos looked at me but had no words. We both reached for the pitcher of water at the same time. He wanted to know the full story.

As soon as I got to the part where I volunteered to draw the culprit's portrait, Carlos ran out of the house. That was the end of the fun and games for Saturday night. Was it the end of our friendship, too?

CHAPTER 11

The next afternoon, I went to the grocery store with my mom.

While she was in the dairy section, I went looking for a new bottle of hot sauce. As I made my way down aisle 6, I saw him: Peter Zorber.

Peter Zorber

Peter Zorber (why is it always the kids we don't like who we call by their full names?) was standing at the end of the aisle, staring me down, almost like he expected me to be there. The Peter Zorber who had to go to summer school. Peter Zorber is big and talks a lot without saying much. Except he never talks to me—he only stares at me like I stole his dog or something.

Peter Zorber is a bully known for giving guys massive wedgies. Really? Wedgies? Who does that? That's a bully move my dad talks about from when he was a kid. Anyway, there is a rumor that he has a list with names on it and he puts check marks next to his victims.

So far, I was not one of them. But would Peter Zorber try it here, at a public supermarket, in front of the ketchup?

My heart rate jumped. I focused squarely on the hot sauce, pretending not to notice as Peter Zorber and his father wandered up aisle 6. I tracked their movements in my side vision. As they passed behind me, I could see Peter Zorber's reflection in the hot sauce.

"You're next, Link," he whispered in my ear as he passed by. I felt it more than heard it, because of his hot reptile breath. "I'll do whatever I have to do to get you before school's done. Be ready."

It was more chilling than being in the frozen-foods section.

I had always been proud of the fact that I avoided him. How much longer could I do that?

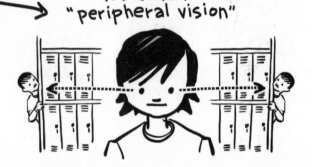

it's called "peripheral vision"

My journal was in the car, and I couldn't wait to draw, so I snuck around the corner, sat on the floor, and used the store sales flyer. On paper, at least, I could defeat Peter Zorber.

When I got home, Andrea was outside, staring at the centipede chalk outline on the sidewalk.

"You wanna play flipdisc?" Since she didn't call me Baby Bro again, I said yes. Andrea liked this game because it brought out her inner scientist. Plus,

It's better than listening to Show-tune Girl practice the same song over and over again.

I couldn't argue with that.

"I think Mothy should be on the Gold Team for Field Day," she said jokingly. "I bet he would be good at the relay. *Killer hornets that disguise themselves as waffle cones!*"

No way I was catching that one.

"If Mothy took my place, it wouldn't be so bad," I said. "*Marshmallow Mount Everest!*"

"Aww," Andrea said. "Well, we'd rather have you than that troll Walker Bundt. *Twenty-four hours when everything is made of chocolate!*"

"Speaking of Walker Bundt, guess who threatened

Walker Bundt

me in the ketchup aisle of the grocery store today? *Three-headed history teacher!*"

I didn't have to tell her that it was Peter Zorber. Everyone knew that Walker Bundt was Peter Zorber's accomplice. He never gave wedgies himself, but somehow he made them happen. Wherever Peter Zorber was, Walker was close by.

"Oh no! I am so glad I'm not a boy." Then came the voice of Amanda from inside the house, calling us in to eat . . . in the form of a song.

Andrea and I ignored her.

"Unfortunately, your other sister has a mad crush on that Zorber creep. I don't get it," she said as she zipped the Frisbee at me. *"Quesadilla with its own elevator!"*

"How is that possible?" I said. *"Pooper-scoopers instead of hands!"*

"Crushes are weird, Baby Bro. I do know that."

"Oh, we didn't hear you the first time," Andrea said as we both headed inside.

CHAPTER 12

It was the Monday morning of the last week of the school year: a worry-free week filled with the anticipation of Field Day and thoughts of summer. Right?

Not for me.

A loud and crowded hallway was the perfect setting for Peter Zorber to sneak up, undetected, and wedgie his victims while they were facing their lockers. I did my locker business quickly and stood with my back pressed up against the door, talking to my friend Felipe on one side and Clay—a kid who smells like he took a bath in vinegar and dried himself off with a used diaper—on the other.

Felipe
wedgied by Zorber while getting off of school bus

Clay
wedgied by Zorber while carrying lunch tray in school cafeteria

Talking to Clay was a small price to pay for not getting humiliated by Peter Zorber in front of the whole school.

There was no sign of Zorber this morning. But in the last few seconds before the opening school bell rang, I saw Andrea running up to me. Great, I thought—she's coming to offer another layer of protection.

Then I saw the scowl on her face. Uh-oh.

"I set Mothy down in my locker, but

when I went to get him, he was gone. Instead, there was this note:"

If you want your project back, Elvin has to meet me in the boys' locker room after school. ALONE.

"Who left this?"

Andrea shrugged. "Mai Lin said that it was Walker Bundt who took Mothy."

In other words, it was Peter Zorber.

"I've been working on Mothy McMothface for a week, Elvin! And I have to turn it in tomorrow. You have to get it back."

"I can't meet him alone! He'll yank my underwear right off my body!"

"Remember last year when you made the toilet into Mr. Trinkle's office?" Andrea asked.

It was one of my finest creations. Mr. Trinkle had commented that he sometimes likes to read when he's in the bathroom, so naturally I turned one of the stalls into an office for him.

"I said that you couldn't have done it, because you were in the lab helping me," Andrea reminded me.

She was right. Principal Weeks probably would have suspended me, but Andrea had covered for me. I owed her a big favor.

"Thanks, Baby Bro."

I had to do this, but it wasn't going to be fun. My body tensed. My teeth clenched. My head hurt. When the bell rang, it felt like the bell at the beginning of a boxing match.

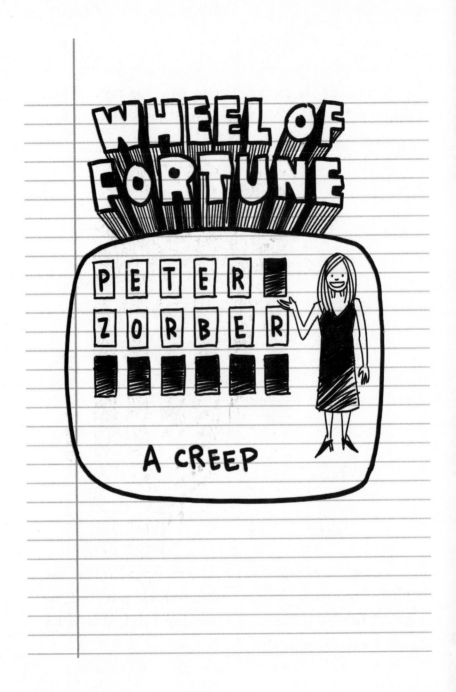

CHAPTER 13

Ten minutes later, I was sitting at my desk, listening to the pitter-patter of the rain on the classroom windows, wondering how I could possibly get Andrea's project back from Peter Zorber without also becoming his last wedgie victim.

The loudspeaker crackled with an announcement.

Carlos! I was so preoccupied with Peter Zorber that I had forgotten about my best friend. He was going to get in trouble because of a drawing I did. Would he ever speak to me again?

The loudspeaker crackled another time.

Elvin Link, please report to the principal's office.

Really? Well, at least I wouldn't have to wait to see whether I still had a best friend.

When I got to Principal Weeks's office, she motioned for me to sit next to Carlos. "I stopped Carlos in the hallway this morning and asked if this was him," she said, holding up my drawing.

"Carlos mentioned that in all the excitement of last Friday, he probably ran into someone, but he kept running and didn't see who it was."

Carlos and I looked at each other. This was an unpleasant moment. If we were playing flipdisc, *getting your best friend in trouble* would be right up there with *screaming jellyfish that pulls your ears off.*

POP!

"Carlos said he was sorry, so I'm not going to prevent him from participating in Field Day," Principal Weeks said. "However, Mrs. English's glasses did break as a result. So I'm asking that Carlos do something for her in return."

"Elvin, I explained to Carlos that you were only being helpful when you volunteered to do that drawing. I know you guys are good friends. There shouldn't be any bad feelings. I'll leave you alone for a minute to talk." She walked across the hall into the teachers' lounge.

"I had no idea it was you!" I blurted out. "I was drawing what they were describing to me. I didn't even know you were there."

"I know," Carlos said frustratedly. "But now I wish

you weren't such a great artist. When you knew it was me, why didn't you draw somebody else?"

"That's not how it works," I said. "But it's not so bad—I mean, she's still letting you participate in Field Day, right?"

"Yeah, I'm glad. But I don't like that suddenly you're narcing me out on stuff."

That's a law enforcement term. A narc is an undercover officer who catches someone doing something illegal and turns them in to the authorities.

"That's not what I was doing," I said. "If you were me, you would have done the same thing."

Carlos paused for a second. "And if you were me, you'd help your friend out. Like, maybe you could draw something cool for Mrs. English? Something that says *I'm sorry*?"

"I don't really think they want to see any more of my drawings. Why don't you volunteer to clean her whiteboard or something?"

"I'm just saying, if you helped out, it would make it even between us."

In the middle of our discussion, Principal Weeks came back into her office. "You guys don't look too happy. Come with me."

What happened next was a surprise: she led us across the hall and into the teachers' lounge.

Students are not allowed in the lounge for any reason. I've always wondered why the teachers' lounge is off-limits. Are there secrets in there? Things that kids aren't supposed to know? Hidden clues to lost civilizations? Trolls? Giant piles of money? I had only gotten momentary glimpses of the teachers' lounge when the door opened, so the principal bringing us inside was a big deal.

It didn't take long for me to realize why students are forbidden to enter: it was kind of a dump. Empty coffee mugs, a bin with a bunch of ratty umbrellas, boxes of half-eaten donuts—who knew teachers were this messy?

There was nothing interesting in the whole room, except for a box against the wall, presumably the Field Day shirts. And there was an electric guitar in the corner, which I assumed was Mr. Trinkle's.

There was also a vending machine.

"Here you go," Principal Weeks said as she handed us each some quarters. "You can treat yourselves to anything you'd like. You can eat it here or at home, but not in class. Our little secret. Deal?"

"Deal!" we both said.

My favorite candy was Caramel Whale Eggs, but I could see that I was not the only one who liked them, because they were sold out. The machine only had the regular chocolate Whale Eggs.

No Cookie Comets, either. I put my coins in and went for the Tolhurst Fudge Crunch Bar. Carlos bought himself a roll of Jelly Jamz.

Carlos and I were eating candy in the forbidden teachers' lounge instead of sitting in class. It's funny how many problems are fixed with candy!

"Here are your hall passes," Principal Weeks said when we had finished. "You can head back to class now."

That's when I remembered Mothy and Peter Zorber.

CHAPTER 14

"**I**'m real sorry, Elvin," Carlos said after I told him my situation. "But I can't help you with Zorber."

"You're just mad about the drawing," I said.

"If I show up with you, you're not getting Andrea's project back," Carlos said. "He'll give you a giant wedgie, and then he'll give me one, just for fun. No way. You should make sure that you're not alone with him."

"Nobody is going to come with me to get wedgied by Peter Zorber."

"You have to make sure someone is there. It would be even better if it was a teacher, maybe."

"There's nobody near the gym after school."

"Draw your way out of it, E. Draw something that will make a crowd observe what you created."

"Are you crazy? And get sentenced to summer school?"

"Make it look like someone else did it! Write someone else's name or something! If anyone can pull that off, it's you."

"But who else in this school draws on walls? They're just going to assume it's me."

"What's going to be easier: talking your way out of that, or talking your way out of Peter Zorber humiliation?"

Certain summer school or total embarrassment: a choice that nobody should have to face. If only I could turn my pen into a magic wand and wave myself to a desert island!

"I'm not showing up with you after school, but if you draw something right now, I'll be your lookout," Carlos said. "Plus, you're the only guy he hasn't wedgied, right? You're kind of the last hope of the fifth grade. If he gets you, he's won."

CHAPTER 15

The plan was hastily thought out and executed. The idea was that I would make two signs

and stick them to the door of the boys' locker room. It was somewhat believable. I would show up with Carlos, and since we couldn't go into the locker room, I wouldn't be alone inside with Peter Zorber. He'd just have to give me my sister's project outside the locker room. There would be teachers walking by, and he wouldn't dare give me a wedgie in front of one of them.

But there were ways this plan could go wrong, including the janitor realizing that the sign was fake and ripping it down before we got there.

Still, it was the best plan I could come up with. I had to make this sign look convincing.

I took some copy paper and a giant marker out of my bag. I placed the paper against the wall and began blocking out the letters while Carlos kept watch.

I had barely gotten started when he shouted "RUN!" and bolted in the opposite direction. I scrunched up the paper, jammed the marker into my bag, and took off. By the time I got to my classroom, I was walking calmly, but my heart was beating outside my body.

So much for that plan. Peter Zorber was finally going to get me, and he would probably get me good.

I didn't even have a chance to enjoy the teachers' lounge candy for very long.

CHAPTER 16

Right before the final school bell rang, the loud-speaker crackled:

I hadn't done anything wrong. What was it this time?

I arrived to find Principal Weeks with her arms folded, a row of angry teachers, and the janitor holding up cleaning supplies. A scene that was as familiar to me as my own face. "We'd like you to come see something," Principal Weeks said.

She and the janitor led us down the hall until we came upon some letters scrawled on the wall:

In the exact spot where I had been drawing the sign. The marker must have bled through the paper and onto the wall. And, of course, I'd never gotten a chance to finish.

"Were you drawing on the walls again?" Principal Weeks asked.

I knew what she meant, but technically, I'd been drawing on the paper.

"I was not."

"I want to believe you, Elvin, but you have drawn on the walls before."

"Honestly, Principal Weeks, if Elvin had wanted to do this, he could have done it way cooler," said a voice from behind us. It was Carlos. He was about to save me. "What the heck is CLOS? It's almost like someone was writing 'CLOSED' and then ran out of time."

Carlos was about to unsave me.

"You mean, someone who was roaming the halls when they should have been in class?" the principal said. "I know two boys who did that today."

We were all but busted.

"Is there a kid named Clos here? At least Elvin's stuff makes sense," Carlos argued.

"Maybe someone was trying to write 'Carlos.'"

"I know how to spell my own name," he said, with less energy this time.

"You have a point, Carlos," replied Principal Weeks.

Carlos was back to saving me again.

"We didn't do it, but how about we clean it up," Carlos offered.

"That's fine with us," the principal said.

I couldn't believe my best friend was signing me up for cleaning supplies AGAIN.

Suddenly we sensed the presence of Peter Zorber. He must have heard the commotion and now stood behind us with a resentful look on his face and Mothy in his hands.

Right behind Peter? You guessed it: Walker Bundt.

I sensed the perfect opportunity. "My sister said you had her project," I blurted out.

"Right," muttered Peter as he reluctantly placed Mothy McMothface near my feet.

"I'm staying here until the wall is glistening,"

interrupted the janitor, handing Carlos and me the towels and spray. "No matter how long it takes you guys to clean it."

We both took the sup-
plies and started scrubbing
the wall. This was not a
fun activity, but it beat getting bullied. Somehow our
botched plan had worked.
We tried not to smile as we
scrubbed, waiting for Peter
Zorber to slither away in defeat.

After we were done and the janitor had left, I heard soft singing from behind me:

I recognized it as the tune that Amanda loved to sing. But it wasn't Amanda singing.

"Looking forward to seeing you at the recital tomorrow night, Elvin," Peter Zorber said before walking away.

This saga wasn't over.

CHAPTER 17

As if the day hadn't ended bitterly enough, my mother made brussels sprouts for dinner. Can somebody explain brussels sprouts to me?

I mean, they're basically miniature lettuce heads. But it's almost like somebody said, "Lettuce is a vegetable, but it doesn't taste horrible enough. How can we make it more disgusting?" They decided to put a head of lettuce in the dryer and shrink it down into a little ball, so there would be no juiciness or crunchiness left in it. Along with the lettuce, they also put into the dryer a bucket of dirt and a pile of year-old gym socks, so that the shrunken lettuce would taste gritty and bitter when it came out.

The only thing that can possibly make brussels sprouts better is—

Well, I haven't figured that out yet. I'm still testing it. "You don't put ketchup on brussels sprouts, Elvin," my mom said.

"*You* don't," I answered.

"Whatever it takes to get 'em down," added my dad. "And we're all getting them down," he continued, looking at my sisters.

Amanda pushed the food around on her plate for five minutes before getting up from her seat.

"Why doesn't she have to finish her dinner?" I asked.

"We told her she could go practice for tomorrow night," Dad said. Amanda sang

while walking away, as if on cue.

"And your project, Andrea?" Mom asked.

"Elvin helped me get Mothy back from Peter Zorber,

that creep. He wants to give him a wedgie. He's basically done it to every boy in fifth grade."

"Who would do that? That's bullying," my mom said.

"Peter Zorber would," replied Andrea.

"Bullies did that a lot when your mom and I were kids," my dad said calmly. "You've got better things to worry about this week than him, Elvin. You just need to finish out the year in a positive way."

"It would be positive if I could do this to him," I said, forking a sprout and drowning it in a pile of sriracha sauce.

"The best thing you can do about bullies is ignore them," my dad said.

"Or report them," said mom.

They both had a point. But I wanted to figure this out on my own.

CHAPTER 18

Did you invite Peter Zorber to the recital tomorrow night?" I asked Amanda as soon as I went upstairs.

"I didn't need to," she answered, seeming annoyed that I would ask. "He wants to be there."

"He likes to hear you sing show tunes about as much as you like Mothy," said Andrea, suddenly appearing with her papier-mâché pet.

"Mothy freaks me out."

"Exactly," said Andrea. "And Zorber's a creep."

"Maybe, but he's a cute creep."

Somehow we all looked at Mothy as if he was going to actually talk.

"Anyway, Elvin, you can just write 'LOSER' on his locker. If he's that big of a creep, you don't have to put up with him," Amanda said.

My sisters weren't in my shoes. I don't think they fully understood what would happen if I wrote on a locker again.

"Mothy has ideas," Andrea said to me as I left the room.

I couldn't sleep that night. Zorber, Zorber, Zorber: the name was haunting me. When I thought about the letter *Z*, I thought it looked like two arrows or two knives thrusting at each other. It was not a fun place to be.

CHAPTER 19

Some days my sisters want to look like twins, other days they don't. Individually, their styles are very different. Andrea is actually the more fashionable dresser of the two; she likes bold prints and bright shoes, whereas Amanda is purely denim and black.

Andrea   Amanda

But on Tuesday morning, it looked like their outfits had been coordinated by Amanda.

Andrea   Amanda

It wasn't an accident.

"What do you think of this, Baby Bro?" Andrea asked me while Amanda was making her breakfast.

She showed me a note she had written:

My voice is shot!
I'm not going to the
recital tonight ☹
But I'll be at
Scooperman Ice Cream
if you want to "stop by"
for a visit ☺
♡-Amanda

"For Peter Zorber?" I asked.

"Duh," she replied. "I don't think he can tell us apart anyway. I just don't know when to put it in his locker."

I thought about it for a second. "It would have to be at the end of the day, right? Or, hand it to him as you're walking away, and don't say anything. He'll see the back of your head and assume you're Amanda."

"Right!"

"What if he tries to talk to you?"

"I won't answer," Andrea said, imitating Amanda's hair flip. "Ms. Godwin told Amanda to limit her chatting today, so she'll be quiet."

"Wow, perfect," I said. Even if this didn't work, I felt a little better knowing that my sister would try to use her twin power to help me out.

"Elvin, this was Mothy's idea."

Right. 😵

Even if Andrea was able to keep Peter Zorber away from the recital, there was still the matter of school. The crowded morning hallway was an environment he used to his advantage, so Carlos and Clay and I hung out in a different area of the school, only running to my locker as the bell rang. Who knew if he'd catch on and set another kind of trap for me?

Elvin Link and Carlos Soto, please report to the principal's office.

"Hello, Elvin," Principal Weeks said matter-of-factly as I walked in. Carlos had arrived before me. "I don't suppose you know why I've called you both here today."

She didn't even wait for our answer. "The Field Day shirts are missing from the teachers' lounge."

"*Missing?*" we replied in unison.

"Come with me." She motioned to both of us and then led us across the hall to the lounge.

"The shirts were here in the lounge yesterday. You might have seen them. They were in a big box that had the Zorber's logo on the side. Zorber's donated the shirts to the school."

Carlos and I looked at each other. Everybody knew that Peter Zorber's father owned a sporting goods store.

Did the Wedgiemaster have something to do with this?

"The shirts were missing this morning. We asked all the teachers as they came in, and none of them said they moved the box. Any idea what might have happened?"

Carlos and I looked at each other and shrugged.

"Mr. Trinkle came to me this morning," Principal Weeks continued. "He told me that he overheard Carlos bragging to classmates yesterday that he'd taken something from the lounge but that he couldn't say what it was."

I turned to look at Carlos. No response.

"When I asked Carlos if this was true, he said yes, but he told me Mr. Trinkle had gotten it wrong. Carlos had actually bragged that it was *both* of you."

That made me angry.

"The only thing we took was candy out of the machine," I protested, "that we bought with the money you gave us."

"That's what I said!" Carlos interjected.

"Did one of the teachers take the shirts by mistake?" I asked.

"Not to my knowledge. I'm not accusing you boys of stealing the shirts. It just seems odd that they are missing."

The lunch bell rang.

RRRRRIIIIIII NNNNGGGG!!!

"I hope you're telling me everything, boys. If you don't know anything about this, you may go."

I started to leave, but Carlos wasn't moving toward the door. "Since we're here already . . . ?" he asked Principal Weeks, and pointed at the vending machine.

She lowered her chin with that look that said, *Are you kidding*? "Don't push it, Carlos," she warned.

I didn't need to spend one second more in the principal's office. However, I did look at the vending machine and noticed that the Caramel Whale Eggs were restocked. They hadn't been there yesterday.

That meant someone had refilled the machine.

"Who refills the vending machine?" I asked cautiously. "There's different candy in there since yesterday."

Principal Weeks walked closer to the machine. She took a deep breath of relief while nodding ever so slightly.

"You're right, Elvin. The person who refills the machine usually comes in after school. She might have been in here when nobody else was around."

"She took the shirts!" Carlos blurted.

"Don't jump to conclusions, Carlos. Let me look into it. You can go now, boys."

CHAPTER 20

As soon as we left Principal Weeks's office, I saw
Carlos turn to me with his hand raised, waiting
for me to complete my half of a high five. "That was
clutch!" he said.

I didn't think there was anything special about no-
ticing candy. Doesn't everybody do that?

"Why are you looking at me like *I* took the shirts?" Carlos said, suddenly annoyed.

"Why did you have to go blab about the candy?"

"Because it was good!"

"I know, but . . ."

"We didn't do anything this time, right?"

"No, but it looks like we could have stolen the Field Day shirts. The *Zorber's* Field Day shirts," I said.

"The vending-machine person did it!"

"How do you know that? At least you didn't volunteer us for something, like you did yesterday," I said, referring to his scrub-the-wall suggestion.

"Wouldn't it be cool if we could figure out who took the shirts? We could be crime fighters, like your dad. We'd be the heroes of the school. Nobody would give us a hard time anymore!"

Principal Weeks poked her head outside the office with that *shouldn't you be getting to class?* look.

"Maybe," I said.

"Flipdisc?" Carlos said. "After school."

"Definitely."

CHAPTER 21

After staying clear of Peter Zorber for a full school day, I met up with Carlos in his front yard. "So the vending-machine person is probably the one who took the shirts, right?" Carlos said. *"Disease that makes your pinkie triple in size!"*

"Why? We don't know anything about her. Or if it even is a her. We should make a list of other options. *A cloud that rains down good grades!"*

"Then it's probably Principal Weeks, right? In those crime shows, it's always the person you least suspect.

Especially if they have power. *Dentist with a turbo-drill!*"

"But they have to have a motive. Why would she want the shirts?"

"Maybe she's trying to frame us," Carlos answered.

"If anyone's trying to frame us, it would be Peter Zorber. Maybe he got someone in his family to do it. *Giant radioactive catfish!*"

"Why would they steal their own shirts that they had just donated? That doesn't make sense. I mean, Zorber is an idiot, but not a thief. *Invisibility potion!*"

"What about one of the teachers? Can't you see Mr. Trinkle trying to look like a cool kid? *Mile-long water slide into a pool of lemonade!*"

our gym teacher

"Or Mr. Vamos," Carlos said, sliding to catch the disc. "Maybe he's got another sports team or something. *Pocket-size laser gun!*"

"Maybe Mr. Torres took them so he can have an unlimited supply of rags to make us clean stuff with," I said, whipping the Frisbee with a purpose. *"Bed full of cockroaches!"*

"Oh! I know who it is!" Carlos said, completely ignoring the majestic arc. "It's Walker Bundt. He knows I can beat him in the beanbag toss, and he's trying to sabotage Field Day! *Fireworks that rain kittens!*"

"I still say it's Peter Zorber trying to sabotage my life. *Double cheeseburger with its own escalator!*"

"What about aliens? They're always trying to take over Earth, right? So they take away the shirts so that Field Day isn't fun anymore. Then they take away pizza and candy and they steal all the computers," Carlos said while unleashing the Frisbee, "so that everything is boring, and we're just sitting around being lazy. Then they reveal themselves and easily come and conquer us! And they start with Villadale!"

"Did you name a flip?" I said. "Or was that it?"

"I guess I forgot."

"I have to get home. Going with my family to Amanda's recital."

"Uh-oh," Carlos said. "Good luck!"

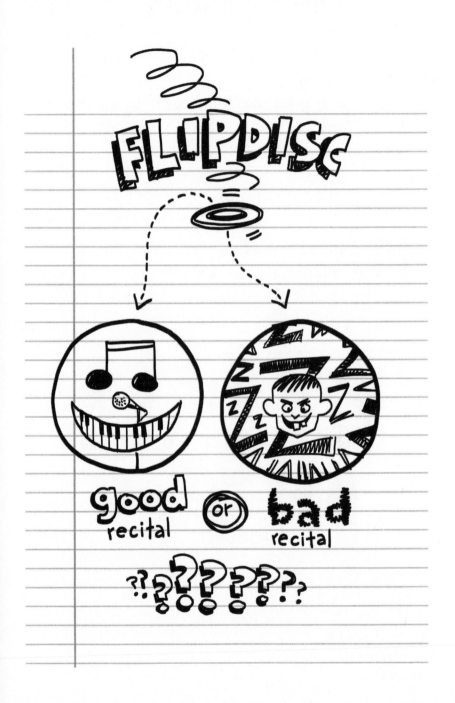

CHAPTER 22

My dad had to work that night, so he dropped me off at the recital hall, where I immediately fired up my Peter Zorber radar.

I couldn't see him, but perhaps he was waiting until the lights went down to make his move. Then I spotted Mom giving a nervous Amanda a last-minute pep talk, with Andrea standing by.

"I think you're good, Baby Bro," Andrea whispered.

"What happened?"

"I came up from behind and handed the note to him in the hallway after the last bell. I waited until I was down the hall a ways, and then I turned around. He was kind of making this face:"

"And then he did this:"

"So I think he bought it."

"You mean you think he'll go to Scooperman?"

"Who cares? If he's really interested in Amanda, maybe he will. But I don't think he'll be here."

I felt a momentary sense of relief. I could actually enjoy the music program, even if I didn't really like hearing girls sing twenty-year-old Broadway songs.

"So he had no idea it was you, not Amanda?"

"No idea," Andrea said.

"No kidding."

With Peter Zorber out of the picture, I could relax. What I enjoyed even more was drawing on some sheet music I found by the piano.

CHAPTER 23

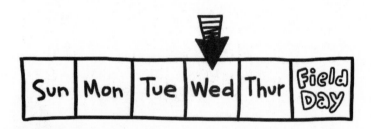

Wednesday morning. I had three more days to keep my guard up against Peter Zorber.

"I've got your back if I see him coming," Carlos said as soon as I met him in the school lobby. "Also, I made this list after what we talked about yesterday. I was thinking: it wouldn't surprise you if Mr. Trinkle *was* an actual alien, right?"

Before I could respond, Principal Weeks appeared.

"Just the young man I need to see," she said. "Can you come to my office?"

For once she was smiling, which was a welcome sight. No sooner had I started to follow her than I caught the death stare of Peter Zorber, who was watching me across the crowded lobby. I felt like Otto if there was a hungry cat licking its chops outside the glass.

Ironically, I was safe in the principal's office. But then Peter turned and started following Carlos down the hall.

That looked like it was going to be trouble.

"I got hold of the woman who fills the vending machines," Principal Weeks said as she motioned for me to settle into a chair opposite her desk. "She claims she saw someone carrying away the box of shirts, and she's willing to come here and describe the person to us. You've got the drawing skills that we need for this, Elvin. Would you be up for doing some detective work today?"

More detective work? Yes, please. *Elvin Link, Detective* had a much better ring to it than *Elvin Link—Detention.*

Even if it meant more time in the principal's office.

CHAPTER 24

After seeing Carlos get followed by the Wedgiemaster, I was eager for lunchtime. Carlos and I usually sit together.

Today, though, he was nowhere to be found. I knew that couldn't be good. Felipe and Clay had no idea where Carlos was, either. But they did a good job of being my lookouts for any Peter Zorber surprise attacks.

As soon as I arrived in my afternoon class, Mrs. English came over to me. "Principal Weeks needs you down in her office," she said quietly. "I'm glad you're doing this, Elvin."

A few minutes later I was back in the principal's office, making another composite sketch. This time I was sitting across from the vending-machine supplier, Ms. Ortiz, who was describing the person who had carried away the box of Field Day shirts.

"Because he was wearing a hat and carrying the box," she explained, "I didn't get a good look at his face."

I lifted my pencil from the page without making a

mark. My drawing was only as good as the witnesses' observations, so this was disappointing.

"If you didn't see the person's face clearly, how do you know it was a man?" Principal Weeks asked.

A good question.

Ms. Ortiz thought for a second. "I suppose I don't, but . . ."

"Why don't you tell me what you did see," I said. The only way out of this problem was putting pencil to paper.

"The person was pretty tall, maybe six foot two," she said. "A big, burly person, someone who would have no problem picking up a huge box of shirts. Wearing jeans and big black boots. The tall rubber kind that you wear in mud or rain."

It had been raining on Monday. A lot of people would have been wearing boots. This didn't get us anywhere.

"The person also had on a brown canvas jacket, pretty beat-up-looking."

Mr. Trinkle was there in the office, nodding a lot and saying "Mmm." I noticed that he was standing in the exact same pose as a basketball trophy on the principal's desk. Was he doing this on purpose? Maybe he *was* an alien, like Carlos joked.

Ms. Ortiz continued. "The box was about three feet by three feet, large, and brown like a paper bag."

"We know what the box looked like," Principal Weeks said impatiently. "What about the person's face?"

"Like I said, the person was wearing a hat, so their face was in shadow. I could see that they had glasses on, but not what kind. Maybe sunglasses. The person did have longish hair coming out from under the hat, down to about here." Ms. Ortiz motioned with her hand around her collarbone.

I had drawn the suspect standing up, but as I thought about how he would have looked carrying the box, I realized that there was one potentially important thing missing.

"Did you see the person's hands?" I asked.

"Yes. Huge hands," she replied with certainty. "They fit around that giant box. Big, sturdy hands, and I don't think he had on any rings or jewelry or anything that I can remember."

She shook her head. "Sorry, I said 'he.' Can we just assume this was a guy?"

"That seems logical now," Principal Weeks said. "And what time were you here?"

"Around four o'clock."

"Steve, let's ask around again. None of the teachers said they were in the lounge at that time, but maybe there's something we're missing."

I visualized all the places around the school and what they would have looked like at 4:00 p.m. I thought about the kids who would have been around the school then.

Then I thought about the person who I see when I leave school every day, whether I walk or ride the bus. "Is the crossing guard still working at that time?" I asked. "Maybe she would remember seeing someone carrying out a large box."

CHAPTER 25

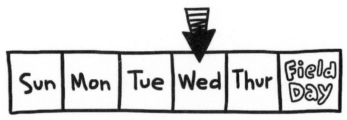

That day, Principal Weeks was waiting for me outside class as the final school bell rang.

"If you can hang around in my office for a few minutes, the crossing guard said she'd describe the box thief for you once she was done with school traffic."

So I found myself in the principal's office again. But doing detective sketches wasn't like cleaning desks. It was almost . . . fun.

I had never seen the crossing guard up close before. Or maybe crossing guards weren't that interesting to me. At least, not as interesting as vending machines with Caramel Whale Eggs.

"Elvin, this is Tina West-Easterly."

"Hi," I said tentatively, not sure of what I just heard.

"Those are my parents' last names!" she said. "You could say I was born to give directions."

Or be confused, I thought.

"So, Tina," Principal Weeks said, "do you remember anything new or unusual about the cars leaving the school parking lot around three thirty on Monday?"

"There was a long silver car, an antique. Driven by the guy with the mustache. I remember that one."

"That sounds like Mr. Vamos, the gym teacher," Principal Weeks said. "He usually drives a small silver car, but he does have a red antique. It was a convertible, right?"

"Yes," Tina said. "He was driving it with the bottom all the way up because it was a nice day."

"You mean the top all the way down," Principal Weeks said.

"Sure. That's what I meant."

"Was there a big box in the back seat, do you remember?"

"Nope, only the guy with the mustache driving in the back seat."

"You mean the front seat," Principal Weeks said.

"Exactly."

Principal Weeks and I looked at each other. Clearly,

the crossing guard had crossed up a lot of things in her mind. I hadn't begun to draw anything yet.

"There was a car I hadn't seen before," she said, squinting her eyes, apparently in order to think better. "It was a truck, actually. A blue pickup. And it did have a big box in the back."

"Tell us more," Principal Weeks said. "What did the driver look like?"

"The driver had shoulder-length hair and very thick glasses. And was wearing a brown jacket and a hat."

"That sounds like Mrs. English," Principal Weeks said. The math teacher often wore a hat to drive back home to her farm because she couldn't fit sunglasses over her thick prescription ones.

"Nope. This was a man."

"Are you sure?"

"Yes. I think I know which teacher you're talking about. She's one of the first to arrive every day?"

"Yes, that's her."

"Well, imagine somebody who looks like her but is a man. Driving a blue truck, not the sporty black car she usually drives."

"That's me with the sporty black car," Principal Weeks said. "Mrs. English drives a small, old yellow one."

"Forgive me if I mix up some of these things," Tina said. "I see a lot of cars enter the school parking lot each afternoon."

"You mean leave the parking lot," Principal Weeks said, barely containing her frustration.

"Sure."

Principal Weeks was done asking questions. "Ms. Tina, nothing you said has made much sense."

"I see a lot of cars, ma'am," Tina replied. "I'm good at cross-guarding. There hasn't been an accident during the sixteen years I have been doing this."

Principal Weeks gave in. "True enough. You've been great. Thanks for trying to help."

After Tina West-Easterly had left, I showed a sketch to Principal Weeks.

"Mrs. English as a man!" she chuckled. "That's spot-on, even if it doesn't help us. Why don't you stop by tomorrow morning before class, Elvin? Let's see if we can come up with more leads. Keep your thinking cap on."

What, exactly, is a thinking cap?

an extra brain?   the "Thinker" statue?   a light bulb?

Whatever it was, I was ready. "Carlos and I had a list of potential suspects. I feel like we can figure this out."

Speaking of Carlos, where had he been all day? I didn't have any run-ins with Peter Zorber, but it seemed like Carlos had vanished. Last time I saw him, he was being followed down the hall by Zorber. And he, as well as pretty much every student, would have left by now. Before leaving school, I checked my locker. I was shocked by what I saw.

CHAPTER 26

What I really needed was some flipdisc time with Carlos, but I had to settle for one of my sisters. Andrea was on dinner duty, so Amanda joined me.

"*Unlimited supply of moisturizer!*" she said dramatically as she spun off a long toss of the Frisbee. She had a good arm.

"I assume that's a good thing?" I said, letting the Frisbee settle into my hand.

"Duh."

"Also, you're supposed to say it right before it lands," I said.

I flicked the Frisbee into the air. "*Carrot peeler for your retina!*" Amanda let it fall.

"I know what you did," she said. "Both you and Andrea. Pretending

to be me so that Peter Zorber wouldn't be at my recital. It was mean. *Milk that's been sitting out in the sun for fourteen days!*"

"He wasn't even there for you," I said. "I know you don't believe that, but it's true. *Snorkel full of scorpions!*"

glonk

"I'd like to see how you feel when you like someone and then I lie to them and say you're sick," she said angrily. *"Diaper full of monkey brains!"*

"Fine," I said. "But I would never like a total jerk. *Bleach milkshake!*"

"It's none of your business who I like. Just leave me alone. *Naked salsa dancing in front of Grandma!*"

"If you wanna hang out with him, I'd be happy to leave you alone," I said. *"Reciting every single line of Shakespeare's plays from memory!"*

"Shark teeth in your face!" Amanda said after chucking the disc right back at me.

At this point neither of us was saying anything that would make the other person want to catch the Frisbee. Finally a voice came from inside the house announcing a more fun activity:

CHAPTER 27

After dinner, Mom handed me the phone.

"Where were you today? You need to see what I found in my locker," I said, explaining the discovery.

Carlos yelled into the phone.

Oh no.

"After Principal Weeks took you into her office, Peter Zorber followed me down the hall and cornered me at my locker. He said I had to bring you to him after school, or else I was going to get a wedgie even worse than the one he gave me last year."

"I remember that. Your underwear ripping was so loud it echoed down the hallway."

"Right. So I took matters into my own hands. Literally. After morning classes I snuck into the up-stairs bathroom and changed out of my underwear."

"That's where you were during lunch?"

"Yep. And by the way, I don't recommend not wearing underwear when your gym class is playing volleyball."

"Ugh," I said.

"So at the end of the day," Carlos continued, "I came around the corner near Peter Zorber's and Walker Bundt's lockers, and I yelled, 'You want my underwear? Here it is!' And I balled it up and whipped it into Peter's face and then took off."

"They didn't catch you?"

"*Sayonara, bullies!*"

"I wish I could have seen that," I said. Although I figured this gave extra motivation for Peter Zorber to make my inevitable punishment reeeally bad.

"So, why were you in Principal Weeks's office again?" Carlos asked.

"I was doing some sketches to help her figure out who took the box of shirts."

"Without me? I thought we were doing that together! I'm running around with no underwear, trying to save you from Zorber, and you're off playing cool school detective without me?"

"We can still do that."

"It's a good thing I didn't accidentally run into anyone again, or you'd be back drawing my mug shot for the principal," Carlos said. "Speaking of which, have you thought of anything cool we can draw for Mrs. English?"

"Haven't thought about it," I said. Carlos still felt like I betrayed his friendship after the ice cream incident. If the awkwardness was a heat rating from a hot-sauce bottle, it would have been at four fires right now.

"Well, we're still doing The Z tomorrow night, right?" I asked. "Maybe we can think of something then."

The Z was a giant entertainment complex that had movie theaters, air hockey tables, and a bunch of video games. But there was one main reason why we went there: laser tag.

If flipdisc was our favorite outdoor game, laser tag was our favorite indoor game. And because Friday was

Field Day, Thursday was technically the last day of school. We had planned a special trip to The Z to celebrate.

"Sure," Carlos said.

Like candy in the teachers' lounge, laser tag had a way of smoothing over all kinds of problems.

Drawing faces based on other people's descriptions was like a tricky puzzle. It was challenging but also fulfilling. I was good at this and felt useful. So after dinner, I went to my room and used the journal to practice for my future.

CHAPTER 28

Sun	Mon	Tue	Wed	Thur	Field Day

Even without mysteries and investigations, the day before Field Day was a strange one. It was like a relaxed version of school. Clay, for instance, smelled just a little bit worse than on a typical day.

Normal Clay

three smell lines

Second-to-last day of school Clay

five smell lines

There wasn't much work to do, so the teachers had us help them clean their classrooms, do little odd jobs, or write short essays about what we had learned over the course of the year. And we were all given year-books, which we spent much of the day signing for each other.

Dear VP:
Can I call you 'Veep'? A lot of people call you that. I don't know if you know that.
It was nice getting to know you this year. You don't talk much, but you seem pretty chill.

Villadale Public
MIDDLE SCHOOL YEARBOOK

I liked it when you let me draw on you. That was super fun, even though some people didn't like it. It would be cool if we could hang out sometime without all these other people around.
I have some good memories from this year, but some bad ones too. I'm mostly just looking forward to the summer. I bet you are, too.
Stay cool, Veep! See you next year. I say that because I am definitely not going to summer school.

— Elvin

We also knew that it was the last we'd see of some of our friends. Kids would be moving on to other schools next fall, and there were a few families who would be moving away over the summer.

It was even sad to think that it was the last time I'd see certain teachers.

I waited for Carlos in the lobby, where Principal Weeks motioned us into her office.

My latest drawing was taped to the wall and being admired by the faculty, although nobody could identify the person.

"It's great work, Elvin," Principal Weeks said. "I think you've found a new job."

I had to admit, it was terrific to be in the principal's office for positive reasons.

"Any more thoughts on the shirts, you two?"

"We got nothing," said Carlos, also feeling important at having been asked.

"That's too bad. I'm going to make an announcement, just in case. Even if we don't find the official gold and blue shirts, we'd still like to have Field Day shirts, so we'll have to figure out something else." Then she reached into a big box and pulled out a white shirt. "We might all wear these."

Carlos and I gasped in unison. It was almost like our hearts had been given wedgies.

It was bad enough that we wouldn't have our regular Field Day shirts. This was ten times worse. Boys at Villadale would rather wear no underwear than a shirt with Zorber's name on it. Except maybe Walker Bundt.

It was all beginning to feel personal. Peter Zorber wasn't just trying to ruin the end of my year, but everybody else's, too.

"Let's hope somebody finds the box," Carlos said, speaking for both of us.

I arrived late for my first class—not a big deal on the last day of school. But all eyes seemed to be on me as I settled into my seat.

"It's a good thing you weren't at your locker," whispered Clay. "Peter Zorber was waiting there for you all morning, with Walker Bundt."

Zorber, Zorber, Zorber. I was tired of hearing that name.

"He was telling everybody he was going to wedgie you on Field Day in front of the whole school," Clay added.

Part of me wondered if I shouldn't just walk up to

him and say, "Go ahead." It felt inevitable, and I was tired of living in fear.

Just then my thoughts were interrupted by the loud-speaker, in what would be the last announcement of the year.

"Attention, all students and faculty: our blue and gold Field Day shirts have gone missing. If anyone knows what happened to the box that was in the teachers' lounge, please come see Principal Weeks in her office as soon as possible. Thank you."

CHAPTER 29

The school day was over.

The school year was over. Mostly. Well, except for Field Day, and me versus Peter Zorber, and an unsolved mystery. Would we be catching the Zorbers in a scheme to steal their own shirts, or would we be helping the Zorbers by finding out who had stolen them?

I stopped by the principal's office on the way to catch the bus home. Several teachers were there. Nobody acted like it was a big deal when I walked in, probably because I had been there so much lately.

"Elvin, no one came forward about the shirts," Principal Weeks said, "so this is what we're going with." She handed me one, as if I had asked.

"Well, at least we have *something*," Mrs. English said.

You could hear more than a few *ugh* reactions from kids passing by the principal's office as they made their way to the double doors.

I might not be able to stop Peter Zorber from yanking me up in the air by my underpants, but I didn't have to wear his name on my chest. So I fought back the only way I really knew how: with ink.

The teachers had almost finished their discussions about Field Day when Mr. Trinkle said, "Hey, Elvin— what are you doing?"

I held the shirt up for all of the teachers to see.

"Love it!" the principal said, followed by the agreement of several teachers.

"Wait!" Mr. Trinkle said. "I have a terrific plan. That is, if you are up for it, Elvin."

CHAPTER 30

"I knew it. Well, maybe you're not really my friend after all, Elvin."

Click.

Silence.

That's how Carlos responded when I told him about Mr. Trinkle's plan.

This was the night that Carlos and I were supposed to go laser-tagging at The Z.

Instead, I was sitting at a table in the school cafeteria and staring at another table, which was piled high with Zorber's T-shirts and colored markers. Mr. Trinkle's plan was that I would replicate the "Zorber's bird" shirt I had drawn in the principal's office over and over again—in gold for every person on the Gold Team, and in blue for every person on the Blue Team.

"These are great, Elvin," Trinkle said. "Your class-mates will love them!"

Maybe, but that news somehow didn't make me happy.

The fluorescent lighting was giving me a headache.

Drawing on top of the Zorber name over and over again was giving me even more of a headache.

Why had I agreed to do this?

At first, it seemed like a cool idea to draw on shirts. But now, as I faced the gigantic pile, it seemed a lot less cool. And it wasn't worth losing my best friend.

I finished my twelfth shirt and then blocked out a

big number 12 on the back in blue marker. I drew it with a shadow behind it, just to make it different.

"Looks great," Mr. Trinkle said.

There were still tons of shirts left to do. This was supposed to be fun, but it felt a lot like detention. In fact, it felt like I was still back there.

The next shirt I pulled toward me was blank. I looked at Mr. Trinkle.

"There weren't enough shirts that say 'Zorber's' on them. The rest are just plain white. We figured you could just write 'Zorber's' yourself," Mr. Trinkle responded.

Oh, heck no. I wasn't going to write the Zorber name on anything.

The only way out of this was the way I got into it: by drawing. But it wasn't quite enough. If this was going to be any good, then someone else needed to be here.

"What's the matter, Elvin? What do you need to keep going? Do you want more pizza?"

"I need to call somebody," I said.

That somebody was Carlos.

"Do you want to play flipdisc right now?" I asked into the phone.

He paused a minute before answering. "I thought you were drawing T-shirts all night," he said sleepily.

"I am."

"I can't help you, E. I can't draw."

"No drawing. Flipdisc. All night."

"I don't get it. How are we going to . . . ?"

"Trust me," I said. "Come to the school right now."

CHAPTER 31

This was how you made Field Day shirts.

It wasn't laser tag. But it might have been better, because it was a game we had invented. A kind of indoor flipdisc that only Carlos and I could play.

Instead of throwing a Frisbee, I yelled out a color and a number. "Gold seventeen!"

And just like in flipdisc, Carlos would yell something back: *"A skyscraper eating doughnuts!"*

And then I'd get busy.

"No way. I want *this* one!" Carlos said. He'd said the same thing after the one before that, and the one before that.

I did half of them in blue and half of them in gold. The markers would run out before our ideas did.

"Blue nine!"

"A robot being stung in the butt by a bee!"

Mr. Trinkle felt like we had out-cooled his original idea, and he wanted to participate somehow. "Mind if I play a little guitar while you guys keep crushing these shirts?" he asked before going down to the teachers' lounge to fetch his instrument. (I knew it was his guitar!)

"Blue twenty-one!"

"A snake backflipping on a skateboard!"

When the night began, I didn't think I could last fifteen minutes. But this was so fun I could draw all night. We were having a blast. And best of all, no one at school would have to wear the plain Zorber's logo on their shirt tomorrow.

"Gold eight!"

"A zombie ninja!"

I also thought that whoever had stolen the plain gold and blue shirts got a raw deal. These would be the ones I'd want to have.

"Blue thirty-six!"

"A pizza-delivery bat!"

Principal Weeks came over and asked if we needed anything. Carlos and I looked at each other. We both had the same answer.

"Nachos. As hot as possible, please."

CHAPTER 32

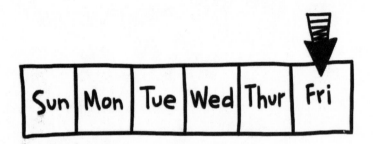

The end of the week had finally arrived.

Because I was up so late, my parents let me sleep in a little longer, and I kind of fell asleep in my cereal. Then I remembered that it wasn't just any Friday. It was

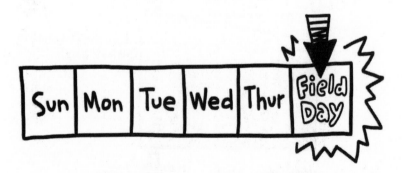

Because this was a day of sports and games, it was one of the rare days when I wouldn't have my backpack of drawing supplies with me. It made me feel naked.

Mom drove me to school, and when I saw the festive sign, it all came to life for me.

But then I remembered what was in store—not only was I going to be That Guy again, but the whole school knew I was going to be That Guy at the hands of Peter Zorber. My attitude changed completely.

Which Field Day was it going to be?

CHAPTER 33

Have you ever seen a pack of dogs let loose inside a steakhouse?

Neither have I. But I think it would be similar to my classmates' reactions to the Field Day shirts.

Mr. Vamos, the gym teacher, lined up all the students and handed out the folded shirts one by one. When the first few kids unfolded them, they responded with excitement. They loved them.

And then Mr. Vamos dropped one.

Instinctively, two kids dove for the shirt. They didn't even know what was on it. One of the kids already had a shirt—he wanted another one. While Mr. Vamos sorted that out, other kids bolted for the carton of shirts that I had drawn. And it became a free-for-all.

In other words, you could say the shirts were a success.

When Mr. Vamos had restored order, he announced that Carlos and I had designed them. There were loud cheers. Everybody on the field was looking at me in awe.

I felt like some people were seeing me for the first time, and not just as that kid they heard being called down to the principal's office. Not just as That Kid from Field Day last year.

Amanda and Andrea pulled out the special letter-*A* shirts I had made especially for them.

I had created a special shirt for Carlos, too, which he proudly revealed.

He also showed the back, which nobody understood except for us. And maybe Principal Weeks.

Field Day could have ended right then and it would have been perfect, as far as I was concerned. But we all knew that there was drama to come.

CHAPTER 34

Maybe the biggest surprise of the day happened in the fifty-skard dash.

Skard is the name that was given to a mysterious animal reportedly seen years ago in the woods of Villadale—described as "part leopard and part kangaroo, with the coloring of a skunk." The animal had run off before the witness could get a second look, and so  because of its supposed speed, there was a race named after it.

Shockingly, this year's winner was Clay. Nobody knew he could run so fast!

Walker Bundt did indeed win the beanbag toss, just barely beating Carlos. Carlos was frustrated. But, like me, he was tired, and because of his personalized shirt, he felt as if he had won Field Day already.

We both thought that flipdisc should be a Field Day sport.

I ran the three-legged race and played dodgeball. I didn't do anything embarrassing. Best of all, Peter Zorber left me alone. But there was still one event to go: the tug-of-Steve.

The tug-of-Steve is similar to a tug-of-war, except that instead of the two teams pulling on a rope and trying to move a flag past a certain point, the rope pullers are trying to move Mr. Trinkle, who perches on a chair attached to the middle of the rope.

Mr. Trinkle reads books (or pretends to), grades papers, writes Post-it notes, and does other ordinary things while the battle is being waged. The joke is that he's pretending he doesn't know there's a tug-of-war going on. It's funny, and annoying, and it makes you want to yank that rope as hard as you can to see him fall off the chair.

The two teams were tied in Field Day wins, which

meant that this event decided everything. And everyone had to participate.

In all tugs-of-war, the bigger and stronger kids think it's better if they're in the back, anchoring the rope with their size. So the bigger and stronger kids—as well as the kids who only *think* they're bigger and stronger—arranged themselves toward the back, telling the smaller kids to go up front.

Walker Bundt made sure that I was sent toward the front of the Gold Team.

The Blue Team did the same thing. Peter Zorber personally organized the lineup of Blue Team members along the rope until they were arranged according to his satisfaction. Peter Zorber, being one of the bigger and stronger kids, would anchor the back of the rope.

Or, maybe on another Field Day he would have. But today he came right up to the very front.

It would have made no sense, except that I was at the front of the line on the opposite side. This didn't pass the smell test.

Peter shot me a devious smile as he grabbed the rope. "Is the Gold Team ready?" he asked, looking at me like he had already won.

"You'd better be ready," said Felipe, who was directly behind me. "No matter who wins, as soon as everybody jumps up and starts celebrating, he's going to wedgie you."

"Did he tell you that?" I asked.

"Basically. The entire school knows he's going to do it."

My whole body tensed. I should never have come to Field Day. I didn't want to quit, but I also didn't want to face my certain humiliation.

I needed my drawing backpack. I wanted to erase everything. This was the moment I had dreaded: it was going to be me against Peter Zorber.

Until it wasn't.

"We should be at the front, too," said a voice from just behind me. It was Amanda, with Andrea right behind her. They left their spots at the middle of the line—where Walker Bundt had insisted they stay—and grabbed the rope on either side of me.

"We got you, Baby Bro," Amanda said quietly into my ear. "We'll fall on you, sit on you, do whatever we have to do to keep Zorber away."

"*Now* we're ready!" said Andrea.

CHAPTER 35

The tug-of-Steve was epic. We were winning. Then the Blue Team was winning. And then us again. And back and forth it went, amid the deafening cheers of both students and teachers. This felt bigger than a game. This was for my pride. My stressed-out body was full of adrenaline.

The rope was at a standstill for a long time, but the Blue Team eventually seized the momentum. We felt them slowly beginning to pull us in their direction. With a wicked smile pasted across his face, Peter Zorber summoned one last burst of strength. I could feel my legs buckle beneath me and my body start to be dragged in his direction. It was almost like he was willing it to happen.

Finally, with a loud "GRAAAAAAHHHHHH!" Peter seemed to single-handedly start a wave of power that sent Mr. Trinkle sailing over the line and onto their side. The Blue Team had beaten us.

However, Mr. Trinkle had been pulled so forcefully that he landed facedown in the mud, right in the pile of Blue Team bodies, his chair on top of him. Peter Zorber, so eager to do what he had set out to do, immediately leaped up in the air with two fists raised in triumph. Unfortunately for him, his shorts had gotten caught on the corner of Mr. Trinkle's chair, and they hadn't joined him in midair.

The Wedgiemaster had pantsed himself in front of the entire school.

He quickly tried to rescue himself, falling down to the ground and wriggling around in an attempt to get his ripped shorts back up to his waist, but the damage was done. He shuffled into the background of the celebration, holding his pants up with both hands.

The Blue Team had won, but it didn't feel like it. It felt like a victory for the Gold Team. It felt like a victory for every kid who had been given a wedgie. And it felt like a sweet victory for me.

As we began to stand up, all eyes were on Mr. Vamos, the emcee of Field Day. It was his job to crown the Blue Team the winners and give out ribbons and prizes. But as he was about to speak, another teacher came and whispered in his ear. Mr. Vamos nodded and stepped back. Somebody else was going to do the honors.

It was Mrs. English.

CHAPTER 36

"Congratulations to the Blue Team for a hard-fought and thrilling victory!" Mrs. English shouted enthusiastically before handing out first-place ribbons to the Blue Team. When you think of Mrs. English, you don't exactly think of sports, so the crowd was somewhat puzzled as to why she'd suddenly taken over.

"I have other prizes to hand out, but first I have an important announcement to make."

There was a long pause and then a sudden mood change. Mrs. English took a deep breath and spoke calmly:

"I'm the person who took the Field Day shirts."

The alternate shirts were such a success that most people had completely forgotten that the blue and gold ones had gone missing. The rousing crowd was suddenly still, with jaws hanging open. Mrs. English? Really?

"Well, technically it wasn't me, but it's someone you might recognize—my son, Ken." Mrs. English stepped aside to reveal a man who had been standing on the sidelines during Field Day. A man who looked a lot like Mrs. English.

"Without my good glasses, I can't see the roads well enough to drive. So he's been driving me to school this week in his truck.

"When I saw the word 'EXTRA' on the box of Field Day shirts in the teachers' lounge, I didn't notice that the words continued on the side to say 'EXTRA-LARGE BOX.' I mistook them for extra free shirts. So, because we needed a temporary home for our hens while we repaired the barn, I told Ken a big box full of soft shirts would do the trick. He came back here on Monday afternoon and took it."

The confused crossing guard had been right: a guy who looked a lot like Mrs. English, in a truck.

My drawing had also been correct. It all made sense now.

Mrs. English went on. "I only realized my mistake the other day and was so embarrassed. The chickens had been using the shirts, so I had them washed and was prepared to return them today. But after speaking to Principal Weeks and seeing what Elvin and Carlos had done with the shirts you're now wearing, I knew that you'd like them better. A lot better." People cheered and clapped, which made me feel great.

Just as she seemed to be wrapping up, Mrs. English added, "And you need to know another important fact: the person who caught us was Elvin Link. Based on a witness's description, he did this sketch."

"While all of you were finishing off the school year and looking forward to the summer, Elvin was busy making the school—and Field Day—a better place. That's why, instead of a prize for Athlete of the Day, I'm giving this shirt to . . .

"Well, let's call him Hero of the Day!"

Mrs. English then pulled out a gold T-shirt, one that had been in the original box, and turned it around to reveal the number 1 on the back. "I think you should wear this proudly. Thank you, Elvin!"

I got more high fives that day than ever before.

Carlos found me in the middle of the crowd. "Guess what? Mrs. English just told me that since we worked hard on the shirts, I don't need to repay her for the glasses."

"Sweet," I replied. "And now I also have a number-one shirt!"

"You've got a long way to go to catch up to me," Carlos said.

As I withdrew from the crowd, I noticed Peter Zorber standing by himself. For once, he was the person who looked like he wanted to disappear. I knew that feeling all too well.

I approached him. "I sort of know what you feel like," I said.

"I'm glad they didn't make you draw a 'LOSER' shirt," Peter said. "I'd be wearing it right now."

I'd gladly draw one of those for you, I thought. But I didn't say this.

"I'm sorry I've been such a jerk to you," Peter said. "To everybody."

"These shirts are incredible, Elvin. I can talk to my dad—I'm sure he'd be happy for you to design a shirt or two that we could sell at the store."

"I could make you a personalized one," I offered. "A big *Z* or something."

It was the least I could do. After all, he was going into summer vacation as That Kid.

CHAPTER 37

Saturday morning. The pancakes were going to taste extra good, no matter what was in them. I was drawing at the table while my sisters were talking away.

"I'm pretty sure it was tomatoes," Andrea declared.

"Tomatoes? They looked like polka dots to me."

They were talking about the pattern on Peter Zorber's underwear.

"They would have been pretty big polka dots. Maybe they were apples or something."

"Of course his underwear would be the goofiest of all," said Amanda.

I stopped my sketching for a minute. "Wait—why did you come and sandwich me yesterday?" I asked Amanda. "Were you trying to protect me from him? I thought he was your crush."

"I thought so, until I found this," she said, extracting a long piece of folded paper from her pocket.

"I hadn't talked to him since before my recital—*ahem*," she said, looking sideways at Andrea. "So on Thursday I asked to sign his yearbook. I kind of grabbed it out of his hand before he could think about it. When I thumbed through the pages, this fell out."

It was The List.

Chad Kirkus	★★★★
Stefan Leandro	★★★★
Elliott Lee	★★★★★
Thomas Lin	★★★
Elvin Link	
Gabriel Loaiza	★★★★★
Troy London	★★★★★
Jason Lu	★★★
Cameron Marte	★★★★
Lucas Maspeth	★★★★★

The only blank was next to my name.

It's almost too bad there wasn't one more day of school, I thought. This deserved a shirt all its own.

"I don't care how cute he is," Amanda said emphatically. "If he's going to be a jerk, especially to Baby Bro, then forget it."

"Who even wants to touch other people's underwear?" Andrea added. "I thought bullies only did that when Mom and Dad were kids."

"Full pancake rights for everybody today," Dad said as he dropped a steaming plate of chocolate chip pancakes in front of me. They never tasted better.

Mom burst into the house from her usual Saturday run. "Are you ready, Elvin? Mrs. Soto is here to take you guys to The Z."

Because we hadn't gotten to go there on Thursday, today was the day. It was even worth missing a few pancakes for.

I ran up to my room to change clothes and thought I noticed Otto facing me, making the shape of the number 1.

If you could give a fish a high five, I thought, I'd be reaching down to Otto right now. But when I looked again, he was back to his normal self.

Another thought crossed my mind as I left my room: A week ago I would have given anything to be in Otto's world. But right now it felt pretty good to be in mine.

© Amy Semple

DREW DERNAVICH is a cartoonist for the *New Yorker* magazine and the recipient of a National Cartoonists Society award. His cartoons have also appeared in many publications, including *Time*, the *Wall Street Journal*, the *Boston Globe*, and the comics anthology *Flight*. He is the creator of the picture book *It's Not Easy Being Number Three* and lives in New York City.

DREWDERNAVICH.COM

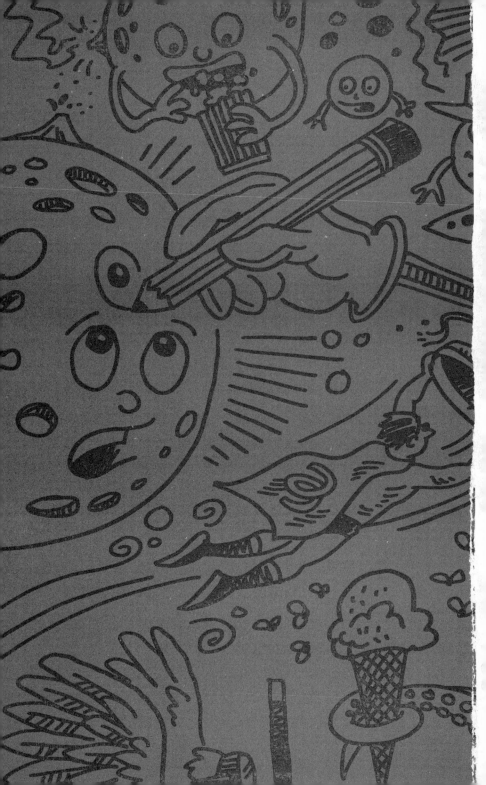